Michael Recycle
and the
Tree Top
Cops

Written by Ellie Patterson
Illustrated by Alexandra Colombo

The beach or the city? The mountains ... a lake?

Even **Michael Recycle** still needed a break!

He flicked through the paper,
just pausing to ponder,
"I'd quite like to visit a natural wonder ...

The Great Redwood Forest!
The world's tallest tree!"

"Yippee!" yapped his dog, Tin Can Stan, happily.

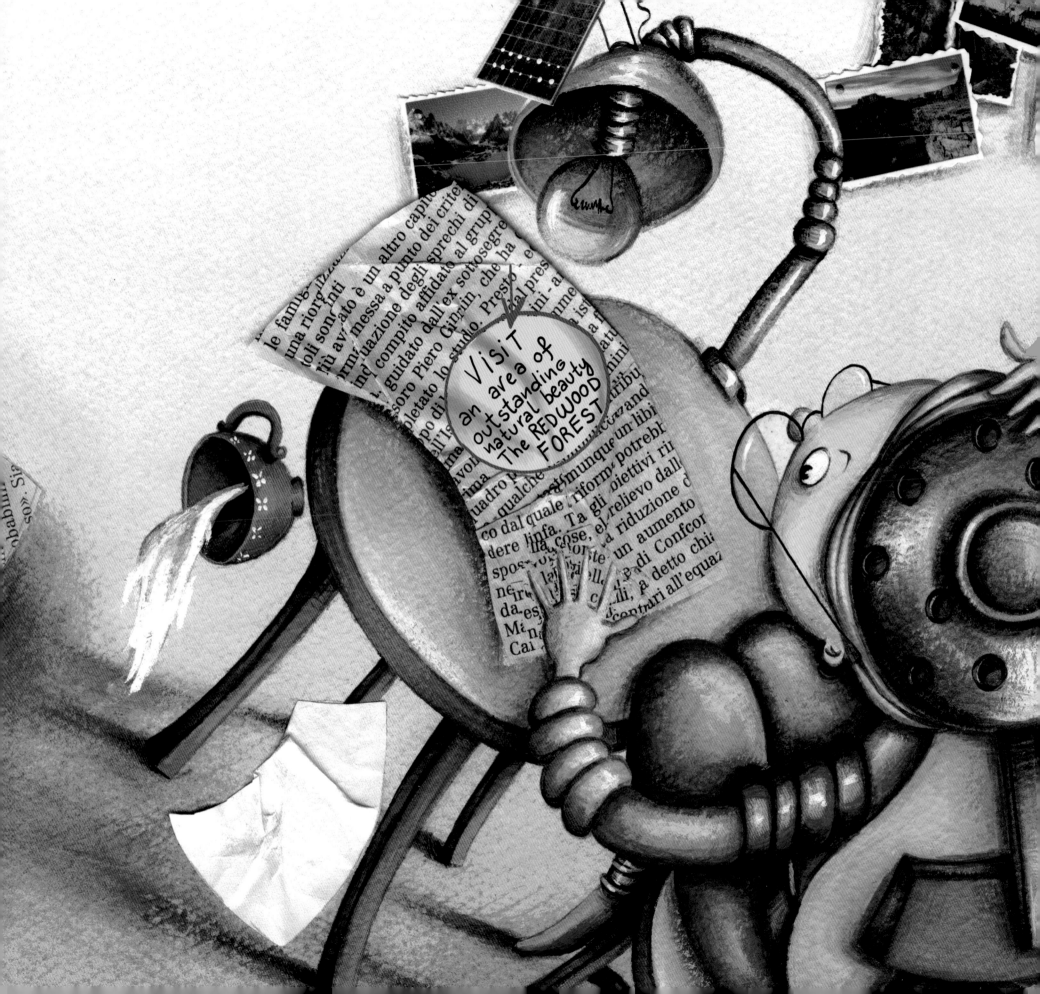

Visit
an area of
outstanding
natural beauty
The REDWOOD
FOREST

But when he arrived at his new destination,
his heart skipped a beat . . .
. . . it was DEFORESTATION!

Bulldozers here and lumberjacks there
were hacking and chopping
down trees everywhere!

"Disaster!" cried Michael. "But who is to blame? I'm Michael Recycle . . . I'll name and I'll Shame!"

And just at that moment, with poodles and pearls, arrived in the forest, all flounces and whirls . . .

. . . two snooty ladies, Celine and Delphine.
Queens of the fashion and magazine scene!

(They needed the trees to feed the machines,
to make millions and trillions of their magazines.)

Michael was angry,

"You must stop this, please!

The air that we breathe
is thanks to these trees!"

But the pair thought that Michael
was simply absurd . . .

. . . and turned up their noses
at all they had heard.

So Michael flew off with a **frustrated sigh,**
then thought up a plan that he wrote in the sky . . .

The Tallest Tree

A huge crowd had gathered
by a quarter past three,
to climb up and meet him
at the top of the tree.

He greeted each one
with a message of hope,
and a helmet, a uniform,
a tool belt and rope.

Early next morning
the lumberjacks came,
and found a BIG problem . . .

. . . but who was to blame?

Michael Recycle
and the new Tree Top Cops!
To save the forest from fashion . . .
they'd pull out all the stops!

We stop tree chops
from the tree tops
we're the tree top cops!

The Tree Top Cops

"Get out of the way!" yelled an angry Celine,
as Delphine drove a **bulldozer** onto the scene.

But the cops wouldn't budge
and continued to hammer,
'til the pair's angry words
were drowned out by the clamour.

Days and weeks passed
in the blink of an eye,
whilst Michael's new friends
built their homes in the sky . . .

There were restaurants and shops
and doctors and schools,
and everyone lived

by the **recycling rules!**

When Celine and Delphine
stormed in looking grim,
(they'd come to see Michael to
reason with him),
a beautiful vision met their
beady blue eyes,
in the green little village
that was built in the skies.

There were girls wearing dresses
hand-stitched with such passion,
all made out of leaves . . .

. . . the **height** of green fashion!

"How chic and unique, this place in the trees!"

"Well here's an idea . . ." Michael said, looking pleased.

So with everyone's help,
it came out one month later . . .

Green Dreams Magazine!

On recycled paper!

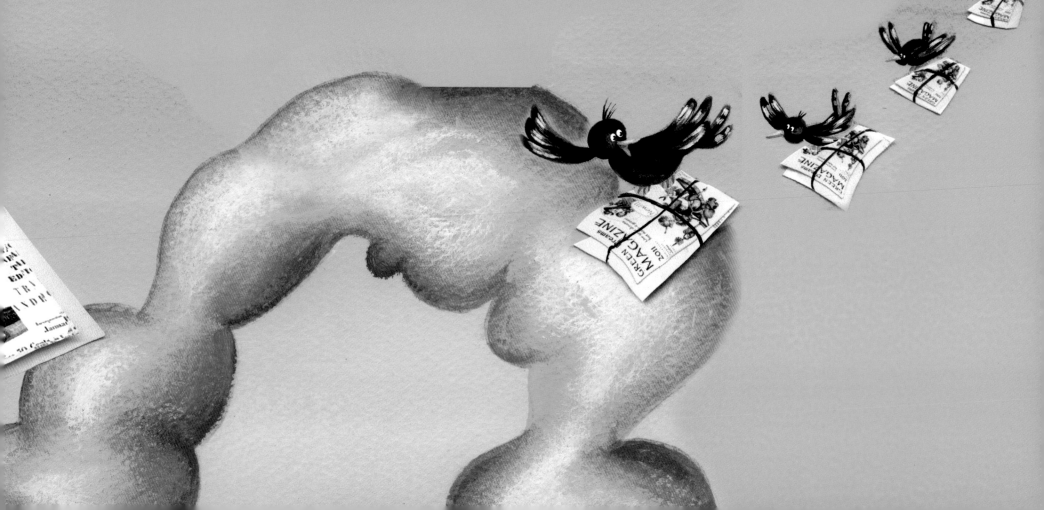

Now thanks to the help of their new magazine,
Celine and Delphine are green-living queens!

On sale now!
The fantastic first issue . . .
. . . re-use and recycle - it's great toilet tissue!

To Molly, Delilah, James and my Editors-at-Large.

E.P.

Per zio Giorgio una persona speciale.

A.C

www.idwpublishing.com
ISBN: 978-1-61377-161-7
15 14 13 12   1 2 3 4 5